Whale Rescue

Look out for more
mermaid adventures:
Spooky Shipwreck
Pirate Trouble
Treasure Hunt

Mermaid Rock

Whale Rescue

Kelly McKain
illustrated by Cecilia Johansson

Scholastic Canada Ltd.

Toronto New York London Auckland Sydney
Mexico City New Delhi Hong Kong Buenos Aires

For my mummy

Scholastic Canada Ltd.
604 King Street West, Toronto, Ontario M5V 1E1, Canada

Scholastic Inc.
557 Broadway, New York, NY 10012, USA

Scholastic Australia Pty Limited
PO Box 579, Gosford, NSW 2250, Australia

Scholastic New Zealand Limited
Private Bag 94407, Greenmount, Auckland, New Zealand

Scholastic Children's Books
Euston House, 24 Eversholt Street, London NW1 1DB, UK

Library and Archives Canada Cataloguing in Publication
McKain, Kelly
Whale rescue / Kelly McKain ; illustrated by Cecilia Johansson.
(Mermaid rock)
ISBN 0-439-93539-3 (pbk.)
I. Johansson, Cecilia II. Title. III. Series.
PR6113.C43W43 2007   j823'.92   C2006-903936-4

ISBN-10 0-439-93539-3 / ISBN-13 978-0-439-93539-5

First published in the UK by Scholastic Ltd., 2005.
First Canadian edition published 2007 by Scholastic Canada Ltd.

Text copyright © Kelly McKain, Prospero Promotions Limited, 2005.
Illustrations copyright © Cecilia Johansson, 2005.
All rights reserved.

6 5 4 3 2 1   Printed in Singapore   07 08 09 10 11

☆ Chapter One ☆

I'm a mermaid, a beautiful mermaid,

sitting on a rock looking pretty!

It was a beautiful day on Mermaid Rock –
just right for playing on the beach or
splashing in the sea. But poor Spirulina had
no one to play with. You see, Coralie and
Shelle were sitting still, combing their hair
and singing mermaid songs.

Spirulina joined in, singing the wrong words on purpose.

Shelle squealed and put her hands over her ears.

"That's not how the song goes!" she cried.

It's too bad I'm so bored, bored, bored!

"Well, I *am* bored, bored, bored," Spirulina huffed. "Why won't you play with me? I want to have some fun!"

"But having fun messes up our hair!" said Shelle.

Just then, a school of silver fish swam by, flashing and glimmering in the water.

"Those little fish will be much more fun than you," said Spirulina, scowling at her sisters. "I'm going to play with *them* instead!"

With that, she dived off Mermaid Rock and disappeared under the foamy waves.

"Watch out you don't get caught in a net!" called Coralie. "There are fishing boats around!"

But Spirulina didn't hear her. She was already far out to sea, following the little fish.

When Spirulina arrived at the seaweed stones, where the little fish played, she got a big surprise. A baby whale was there too!

"Hello, I'm Spirulina," said Spirulina.

"I'm Splosh," said the baby whale. "I followed the little fish. Come on, let's play!"

The little fish let Spirulina and Splosh join in all their games.

They played Sleeping Lionfish…

…Fish and Shark…

…and Pin the Seaweed on the Snapper.

They had so much fun! But then Splosh

stopped playing.

"What's wrong?" asked Spirulina.

Splosh looked up and down. Then he started to cry. "I can't see my mummy," he wailed. "I'm lost!"

☆ Chapter Two ☆

Spirulina put her arm round Splosh. "Don't worry," she said. "We'll find your mummy. Where were you before you followed the little fish?"

"I can't remember," Splosh sobbed. "And I forgot to tell her where I was going!"

"That's okay, I'll
think of something,"
Spirulina promised.
She thought
really, really
hard until…

"I've got it!" she cried.
"We'll sing the whale song!"

"What's that?" asked the littlest little fish.

"It's a special song that whales can hear
from far away," Spirulina explained.
"Splosh's mummy will hear us
and come to find him."

"Hooray!" cheered Splosh.

So they all sang the whale song.

Whales, whales, out at sea,
hear this song and come to me!

Then they waited…but Splosh's mummy
didn't come.

"Once more!" shouted Spirulina. "As loud
as you can!" Everybody sang until they were
about to burst.

Suddenly, a huge
shape came gliding
towards them.

"Look, Mummy's coming!" cried
Splosh in delight.
The little fish all cheered and
hugged Spirulina.

But wait…something was wrong.

"That's not my mummy!" Splosh gasped.

"That's a fishing
boat!"

A fishing net was trailing behind the boat.

Everyone screamed and tried to swim away,

but it was too late.

The net scooped them
all up!

"Quick, everyone! Wriggle!" called the littlest little fish.

All the little fish wriggled and wriggled until they had wriggled right out of the net.

Spirulina and Splosh wriggled too, but they were just too big. In desperation, they beat their tails up and down.

The fishing boat rocked from side to side and the net started to fray.

"We're nearly free!" cried Spirulina. "Keep going!"

The threads of the net were just about to break when…

"Argghhhhhh!" they screamed.

The net was wrenched out of the water.

They were trapped!

⭐ Chapter Three ⭐

When the three fishermen saw the net,
they were amazed.

"What's this? A real live mermaid and
a baby whale!" gasped one.

"Let us go!" shouted Spirulina, still
struggling.

The big fisherman leaped
forward and started to
untangle the net. He
had red hair just
like Spirulina. She
grinned at him
and he grinned back.

"Leave her there, Softie Bill!" shouted one
of the other fishermen as the third put down
the anchor. "People will pay a lot of money
to see a mermaid. We'll show
her at fairs. We'll make a
fortune, won't we,
Fastnet?"

"Aye, Fisher," said Fastnet. "She'll only need a tiny tank. Or even just a large bucket."

Spirulina shuddered. "You can't do that to me!" she shouted.

"Oh, yes we can," said Fisher and Fastnet, chuckling. They lowered the net onto the deck and pulled Splosh out.

Spirulina's heart leaped. "At least they're letting you go, Splosh!" she cried. But they didn't. Instead they tied him down to the deck with a strong rope.

"That'll stop you rocking the boat," snapped Fisher.

"Oh, please don't do that!" bellowed Softie Bill. "He's only a baby!" "Shush, you big lump," snarled Fastnet. Softie Bill hung his head.

Then Fisher and Fastnet tied Spirulina to the boat's mast. "You'd better stay put too, mermaid – or else," sneered Fastnet.

Spirulina was furious. But she knew she had to escape and save Splosh.

"Come on, Fisher. Let's go below deck to find something to put that pesky mermaid in," said Fastnet. "Softie Bill, you guard her."

Softie Bill came and stood next to Spirulina. Spirulina thought for a moment.

Then she smiled at him. "You're not a softie," she said. "I think you could be

quite brave, if you tried."
Softie Bill blinked at her.
"Really?" he asked.
Spirulina nodded.
"In fact, you could be
brave right now, by
helping me to escape."

For a moment, Spirulina thought Softie
Bill was going to help. But then, Fisher and
Fastnet reappeared on deck with a large
bucket. Softie Bill cast a nervous glance at
them. "I can't,"
he mumbled.
"I'll get
into
trouble."
   "Well, at least
help poor Splosh," said
Spirulina quickly. "Whales
don't like being out of the ocean.
He needs to stay nice and wet. You could
use that bucket to pour water over him."

"Hey, Softie, stop talking to that mermaid and make us some tuna sandwiches!" shouted Fastnet.

Softie Bill gave Spirulina a sad look and scurried away. But before he went below deck he sneakily poured a bucket of water over Splosh. Spirulina smiled to herself and started planning her escape.

☆ Chapter Four ☆

Splishity-splash! Splishity-splash!

What was that? Spirulina listened hard...

The little fish! They must be swimming around next to the boat.

"Pssst! Little fish!" hissed Spirulina. "Is that you?"

"Yes," said the littlest little fish.

"Oh, good," whispered Spirulina. "I need your help. Can you distract Fisher and Fastnet for me?"

"No problem," whispered the littlest little fish. "This will be fun!"

The little fish swam around just out of reach, shouting rude things and blowing raspberries at Fisher and Fastnet.

"Grrr," growled Fisher. "We'll make you all into sandwiches!"

Spirulina set to work.
First she wriggled
her hand down
to her tool belt.
Then she grabbed
her saw and started
cutting through the net.
It took a long time but, finally, she
freed herself and crept across the deck.

"Yay!" cried Splosh. "I'm saved!"

"Shhh!" hissed Spirulina.
"They'll hear us!"

Spirulina started to saw through Splosh's ropes, but they were just too thick.

"Oh no!" wailed Splosh, starting to cry again.

Splosh's crying made Fisher and Fastnet turn around. "Hey! Stop that!" they shouted, lumbering down the deck after Spirulina. Fisher grabbed her but she slid through his fingers and dived into the sea.

"Follow me!" she called to the little fish. "Back to the seaweed stones!"

When they arrived, Spirulina found the snapper. "Please can you help us?" she asked, very politely.

"No way!" grumbled the snapper. "Not after you tried to pin the seaweed on me!" He snarled and snapped his teeth at her.

Spirulina leaped backwards. "Oh, please don't bite me!" she cried. "I'm sorry about the seaweed. We really, really need you."

"Really?" said the snapper, peering at her.

"Oh yes," said Spirulina. "We need you because you're great at biting."

The snapper looked pleased. "I *am* great at biting," he said. "Okay, what do you want me to do?"

Once Spirulina had explained, they all swam back to the fishing boat.

Spirulina climbed up the side, with the snapper hidden in her tangled hair.

Softie Bill was still below deck, but Fisher and Fastnet were leaning over the side of the boat raising the anchor. The little fish swam over to them and started to shout rude things.

Spirulina took a deep breath, crossed her fingers for luck and hurried over to Splosh.

☆ Chapter Five ☆

Chomp! Chomp! Chomp!

The snapper's teeth flashed like steel. In two seconds flat, he had bitten through Splosh's ropes!

"Wow! Thanks!" whispered Spirulina.

"My pleasure," said the snapper, flipping himself back up into her hair.

Spirulina was just trying to push Splosh over the side of the boat when Fisher spotted her.

"Oh, no you don't!" he snarled, running over and grabbing her. Spirulina fought back with all her might but this time she couldn't get away.

Splosh began to thrash around, making the boat rock…until Fastnet dashed over and sat on him.

They were well and truly caught. But
Spirulina refused to give up. "Quick,
everyone, sing the whale
song!" she cried.

Whales, whales,
out at sea, hear this song
and come to me!

She started
to sing and
the little fish
and Splosh
joined in.

"Be quiet!"
demanded Fisher. He reached out to put
his hand over Spirulina's mouth.

"Oooooowwwww!" he screamed.
The snapper had swung down
from Spirulina's
hair and
chomped on
his hand.

Fisher staggered backwards and Spirulina was free.

"Wow, thanks again!" she gasped.

"No problem!" said the snapper proudly.

"Keep singing, everyone!" cried Spirulina.

Just then, Softie Bill appeared on deck with a plate of sandwiches. He blinked at them in amazement.

"Help us, Softie Bill!" Spirulina begged. But Softie Bill shook his head. "I – I – I'm not allowed," he mumbled nervously, glancing at Fisher and Fastnet.

"Oh, please," she cried. But Softie Bill stayed silent.

They sang as loudly as they could. But Splosh's mummy *still* didn't come. Spirulina's heart sank. It was hopeless…but then…

A booming voice joined in. It was Softie Bill!

"Hey, Softie, stop that right now!" ordered Fastnet, but Softie Bill just clenched his fists and kept on singing. His bellowing voice boomed through the air.

Suddenly there was a rumbling and a rocking and a roaring. The boat began to shake.

"Uh oh!" said Fisher.

"Yikes!" said Fastnet.

WHOOSH!

The boat was tossed right up out of the
water. Spirulina and Splosh and the
fishermen flew through the air.

"Arrggghhhh!"

SPLASH!

They crashed into
the sea. Splosh's
mummy had
come at last.

"You found me!" cried Splosh, swimming to her side.

"I heard the whale song," she said, hugging him tight. "Oh, you gave me such a fright! I've been looking everywhere for you! Never *ever* swim off on your own again!"

"Don't worry, I won't!" promised Splosh.

The three fishermen thrashed about helplessly in the water. Spirulina rescued Softie Bill and put him back in the fishing boat.

"Help! Help! Please save us too, kind mermaid!" spluttered Fisher.

Spirulina scowled. "Why should I?"

"We'll change our ways!" gurgled Fastnet.

"I'll make sure they do," called Softie Bill. "I'm taking charge of this boat. And from now on, my name is Brave Bill. Got that?"

"Yes, Captain Brave Bill," cried Fisher.

So Spirulina rescued them too.

"Well done, Brave Bill," said Spirulina.
"Without your booming voice, Splosh's
mummy would never have heard us."
Everyone cheered for Brave Bill.

Brave Bill grinned. "Thanks for making me
brave," he said. Then he sailed the fishing
boat away, waving from the helm.

"Thank you for saving my baby, Spirulina,"
said Splosh's mummy, who was called Splash.
Spirulina blushed. "It wasn't just me," she
insisted. "It was all of us working together."

"Would you like a ride home?" asked Splosh.
"Yes, please!" said Spirulina, beaming.

Coralie and Shelle could hardly believe
their eyes when Spirulina came riding up
to Mermaid Rock on a whale!

"Spirulina's singing saved me from the
fishermen," Splosh told them. He thrashed
his tail in delight, drenching them all.

"Arghhh!" cried
Coralie and
Shelle.

"Oops,
sorry!"
said Splosh.

Spirulina just laughed and shook her tangled hair. "Will you play with us?" she asked.

"Of course we will," said Coralie.

"After all, we can't get any messier!" added Shelle.

They played with Splosh and his mummy until sunset.

Then, tired and happy, the three mermaids said goodbye to the two whales. They stood on Mermaid Rock, waving and waving. Soon all they could see were two tails, one big and one little, arching on the horizon. Spirulina smiled to herself and wondered what her next adventure would be.